KUNG POW CHICKEN★

BOK! BOK! BOOM!

Cyndi Marko

BRANCHES

SCHOLASTIC INC.

For Kaelen,
who's a tough egg to crack

No part of this publication may be reproduced, stored in a retrieval system, or transmitted in any form or by any means, electronic, mechanical, photocopying, recording, or otherwise, without written permission of the publisher. For information regarding permission, write to Scholastic Inc., Attention: Permissions Department, 557 Broadway, New York, NY 10012.

Library of Congress Cataloging-in-Publication Data
Marko, Cyndi, author.
Bok! bok! boom! / by Cyndi Marko.
pages cm. — (Kung Pow Chicken ; 2)
Summary: Superheroes Gordon Blue and his brother Benny must rescue an opera star from the evil Dr. Screech before he turns her super high voice into a supersonic weapon.
ISBN 0-545-61063-X (pbk. : alk. paper) — ISBN 0-545-61064-8 (hardcover : alk. paper) — ISBN 0-545-61392-2 (ebook) 1. Superheroes—Juvenile fiction. 2. Chickens—Juvenile fiction. 3. Rescues—Juvenile fiction. 4. Supervillains—Juvenile fiction. [1. Superheroes—Fiction. 2. Chickens—Fiction. 3. Rescues—Fiction. 4. Supervillains—Fiction. 5. Humorous stories.] I. Title.
PZ7.M33968Bo 2014
[E]—dc23
2013027608

ISBN 978-0-545-61064-3 (hardcover) / ISBN 978-0-545-61063-6 (paperback)

12 11 10 9 8 7 6 5 4 3 2 1   14 15 16 17 18 19/0

Printed in China.
First Scholastic printing, April 2014

TABLE OF CONTENTS

kite

lunch box

city of
Fowladelphia

glasses

comb

beak

wattle

wattle

tail feathers

Gordon Blue seemed like an ordinary chicken.

He was in second grade at an ordinary
school in the ordinary city of Fowladelphia.

And he had an ordinary family. (Sort of.)

But Gordon had a <u>super</u> secret.

When Gordon was younger, he and Benny fell into a vat of toxic sludge at their Uncle Quack's lab.

The toxic sludge was no ordinary toxic sludge. It had given Gordon superpowers.

Gordon promised only to use his superpowers for good.

Uncle Quack had promised to keep Gordon's secret. But it was still <u>super</u> tricky to keep the secret from Gordon's mom.

Gordon had a super suit. He kept it hidden in his lunch box. And he carried his lunch box everywhere. Whenever he squeezed into his super suit, he became Kung Pow Chicken.

Last week, Kung Pow Chicken had saved the chickens of Fowladelphia from a bad guy called Granny Goosebumps.

THE FOWL

HOODED HERO SAVES CITY

A new hero, Kung Pow Chicken, stopped bad guy Granny Goosebumps. The grumpy granny sold glowy cookies that made many chickens lose their feathers. Then the granny sold sweaters to those birds-in-the-buff! Kung Pow Chicken beat Granny Goosebumps in a battle. And Professor Quack Blue made a glowy milk to regrow the naked chickens' feathers. Now the granny does her knitting in jail.

When asked for a comment, Granny Goosebumps said, "I wish I were in Florida."

TIMES

FAMOUS SINGER IN TOWN

Miss Honey Comb is well-known for her super-high singing voice. She will be singing at the Fowladelphia Opera House. Get tickets today!

BIG-SHOT SOUND SCIENTIST IS BACK

Dr. Screech grew up in Fowladelphia, and has returned to the city this week. Dr. Screech said he plans to go to the opera. And he said he might like to see what's shaking at the Public Library, too.

Now Kung Pow Chicken was totally famous. But being a famous superhero wasn't easy.

Gordon couldn't tell any of his friends his <u>super</u> secret.

You're grounded!

Fighting bad guys sometimes made him late for dinner.

And a snoopy reporter named Sam Snood just never got his story right.

HELPFUL HERO OR TROUBLE IN TIGHTS?

Sam Snood Junior Reporter

Kung Pow Chicken may wear a super suit, but he has super-bad manners. He is rude to grown-ups — just ask Granny Goosebumps!

There is a reward if you can tell me Kung Pow Chicken's real name!

$$ REWARD $$

Tonight, Gordon would have to be just an ordinary chicken. He had to go with his family to the <u>la-dee-da</u> opera to hear overstuffed chickens sing.

SQUAAAAAAAAAAK!

Honey Comb sang and sang. But Gordon had
no clue what she was singing about.

Gordon didn't like the opera. He had never been so bored in his whole life. Then he spotted Sam Snood.

Honey Comb had been singing <u>forever</u>.
At last, the curtain dropped and the singing
stopped.

Yay! It's over!

This is just a quick
break to grab a
snack, Gordie. We'll
get to hear more
singing after!

Mrs. Blue went to the snack counter. Uncle Quack, Gordon, and Benny were waiting for her when a strange chicken walked over. A <u>very</u> strange chicken.

THE SODA FOUNTAIN OF THE OPERA

PROFESSOR QUACK! I'VE HEARD SO MUCH ABOUT YOU!

I AM DR. SCREECH.

A doctor? I fell off my Big Wheel today. Could you look at my boo-boo?

Ham and eggs! Is that his inside voice?

Gordon, Dr. Screech isn't <u>that</u> kind of doctor. He's a scientist, like me!

Then Dr. Screech said he had to go back to his seat. Gordon's tail feathers began to wiggle.

Gordon and Benny looked around. They didn't see anything out of the ordinary.

My birdy senses must be on the fritz. I don't see any bad guys up to no good.

Then Mrs. Blue said it was time to go back to their seats. Soon, Honey Comb was singing again. Gordon's tail feathers were still wiggling, but everything seemed fine.

Suddenly a giant hook came down. It snagged Honey Comb, yanking her up into the air.

Gordon's birdy senses almost shook him out of his seat. Mrs. Blue fainted. Uncle Quack caught her just in time.

Bad guys needed catching. A chicken needed saving. Gordon grabbed his lunch box. Then he and Benny looked for a place to hide.

Gordon and Benny changed into their super suits.
Now Kung Pow Chicken and Egg Drop were
ready to get cracking.

The superheroes quickly climbed up a ladder to the roof. They peeked out. Honey Comb was still dangling from the hook. And the hook was dangling from a giant crane arm. Dr. Screech sat at the controls!

SQUAAAAWK! Help!

TRAPDOOR

22

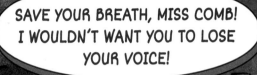

SAVE YOUR BREATH, MISS COMB!
I WOULDN'T WANT YOU TO LOSE
YOUR VOICE!

Kung Pow Chicken and Egg Drop ducked
back down.

Then Kung Pow Chicken took a deep breath.
He jumped out onto the roof. He was ready to
kick Dr. Screech in the wattles.

Dr. Screech held a funny-looking cone up
to his beak. It was a megaphone and it made
everything he said <u>mega</u> loud.

MY MEGA-MEGAPHONE
MAKES MY VOICE MEGA
LOUD. IT ALSO FLINGS
MEGA TRAPS!

SQUAWK!

The heroes were trapped!

Kung Pow Chicken used his Power Peck to break free. But it was too late.

Dr. Screech slung Honey Comb over his shoulder. Then he zipped away.

Come on!
After them!

Kung Pow, stop!
You'll slip and fall!

RIINNG!

Kung Pow Chicken's Beak-Phone was ringing.
It was Uncle Quack.

Boys, your mom is awake! She wants to know where you are! Come back! Quick!

But what about Honey Comb?

We'll have to follow Dr. Screech later. Come on!

Kung Pow Chicken and Egg Drop climbed down from the roof. Then they changed back into their fancy clothes.

They found their mom by the snack counter.
That reporter Sam Snood was asking her some
questions.

Gordon quickly filled Uncle Quack in on what
had happened on the roof.

Boys, this is serious. Sound is a kind of energy. That must be Dr. Screech's bad-guy power.

Sound energy? What do you mean?

I liked it better when the bad guy just baked cookies.

Sound is made of waves. If you can make a loud enough noise, then the sound waves can shake things to pieces.
Sound wave
Ham and eggs! Honey Comb was voted the loudest singer five years in a row! Dr. Screech could use her voice to shake the city to bits!
Uncle, can you make anything to help us? We need to follow Screech. And that zip line is our only clue!

Just then, Mrs. Blue marched over to where the boys were talking with Uncle Quack.

Mrs. Blue gave Gordon and Benny kisses.
Then she sent them off with their Uncle Quack.

oon as they got to the lab, Gordon and
ut on their super suits. Uncle Quack gave
gadget to help them follow Dr. Screech's

t
t
hile
e.

LET'S GET CRACKING!

To the
Beak-Mobile!

Pow Chicken took out his phone. He
the AUTO-BEAK button to make the
obile come to the lab.
he pedaled back to
ra house to pick up
ech's trail.

The opera house looked dark and empty—and locked. Kung Pow Chicken and Egg Drop crept around the building. They looked for a way up to the roof.

I don't see a way up. Do you?

No. Maybe on the other side?

They started to climb up the waterspout. But Kung Pow Chicken saw an itsy-bitsy spider.

Kung Pow Chicken flung the Beak-A-Rang up to the roof. Then he and Benny started climbing.

Boy, this is hard work!

At least you have arms!

PUFF PUFF

Finally, they reached the roof.

Kung Pow Chicken thought Sam Snood was a real pain in the beak. But he did not have time to talk to Sam Snood now. There was a bad guy on the loose.

Kung Pow Chicken hung Uncle Quack's gadget over the zip line. Then, with Egg Drop holding on tight, he zipped!

ZIP!

The heroes zipped
past many streets,
and over many rooftops,
until they came to
the end of the line.

Dr. Screech was there waiting for them. He squawked into his Mega-Megaphone. The loud mega sound waves blasted Kung Pow Chicken and Egg Drop right off the roof.

Kung Pow Chicken flung the Beak-A-Rang.
He caught Egg Drop just in time!

Kung Pow Chicken was no birdbrain. He knew what to do. He sucked in a super breath and—

Dr. Screech was blown backward off of the
rooftop. But he flung his arms and legs out wide.

Dr. Screech was wearing a flight suit!

YOUR BOK IS A REAL DOOZIE, KUNG POW CHICKEN!

WITH YOUR BOK, I COULD BE THE BIG CHEESE!

I eat cheese for breakfast!

You're both pretty cheesy.

WHOOSH!

Then Dr. Screech flew away.

Kung Pow Chicken slid to the ground. He was beat. <u>He</u> couldn't fly like Dr. Screech. Kung Pow Chicken zipped the Beak-A-Rang into his belt.

Now what?

Now we go home. Mom said we had to be back first thing in the morning.

The sleepy heroes were ready to go home. Kung Pow Chicken pressed the AUTO-BEAK button on his Beak-Phone. The Beak-Mobile pulled up.

Gordon Gets His Wings

6

Gordon took a quick power nap when he got home. He woke up feeling like a new chicken. But while he was eating breakfast, he saw the front page of his mom's newspaper. . . .

THE FOWL TIMES

FAMOUS SINGER CHICKNAPPED!

by Sam Snood

Honey Comb was hooked from the Fowladelphia Opera House last night by new bad guy, Dr. Screech. Opera-goers saw Kung Pow Chicken with Dr. Screech. Where is Honey Comb now? Did Kung Pow Chicken help Dr. Screech snatch the singer?

Only bad guys wear masks! The reward for telling on Kung Pow Chicken has doubled. Just tell me.

$$REWARD$$

Gordon almost choked on his cornflakes after reading what Sam Snood had written about him.

Mrs. Blue handed Gordon a glass of water.
He took a sip. Then Benny asked if they could go
back to Uncle Quack's lab for the day.

Gordon and Benny headed straight for Uncle Quack's lab. They hoped he had been able to find out more about Dr. Screech. They had to find a way to rescue Honey Comb and save the city! But this bad guy was a tough egg to crack.

As Gordon and Benny passed chickens on the street, they heard mad mumbles.

We want a hero, not a super zero!

Kung Pow Chicken chicknapped Honey Comb?!

Kung Pow Chicken looks like a super doofus in this photo!

AL'S FOOD and STUFF

NEWSSTAND

Gordon was upset by what the chickens were saying. But Benny reminded him that a true hero helps out—no matter what other chickens say about him.

When Gordon and Benny got to the lab,
Uncle Quack had a lot to tell them.

Dr. Screech was testing a new invention at Mad Scientist School. It was called the Cone of Silence.

But Dr. Screech stayed inside the quiet cone WAY too long! It scrambled his brain!

Now he gets upset when things are too quiet.

That explains everything!

And Mom thought <u>Uncle Quack</u> was cuckoo.

Gordon and Benny quickly changed into their super suits.

Kung Pow Chicken and Egg Drop followed Uncle Quack up to the roof. Uncle Quack had made new <u>super</u> gadgets for his nephews. He gave them each a pair of Safe-T-Muffs™.

These Safe-T-Muffs™ will protect your ears from loud sounds—like that loud screeching.

SCREEECH!

Huh?

What?

Then he gave his nephews a hang glider.

Now the superheroes were ready to fight the bad guy.

Dr. Screech's voice boomed through the air.
The city thundered with noise. Windows rattled!
Chickens bokked! Car alarms beeped!

Kung Pow Chicken took a deep breath. He
gritted his beak. Dr. Screech didn't scare <u>him</u>.

Kung Pow Chicken landed the Chicken-Wing™ next to Dr. Screech's hideout. It was a noisy building. The heroes slipped in the front door and put on their Safe-T-Muffs™. Kung Pow Chicken flashed his Drumsticks of Doom.

EXIT

STAIRS

They tiptoed from room to room, and floor to floor, and finally to the roof.

Kung Pow Chicken spotted Honey Comb. He rushed right over to her. Honey Comb tried to warn him.

But it was no use. Kung Pow Chicken couldn't hear a thing while wearing his Safe-T-Muffs™. A big claw snapped shut around him!

What do you want with us, Dr. Screech?
I PLAN TO WRECK ALL THE QUIET PLACES OF THE WORLD! AND I'M GOING TO START BY USING YOUR VOICES ON MY ULTRA-MEGA-MEGAPHONE TO SHAKE THE FOWLADELPHIA PUBLIC LIBRARY TO ITTY-BITTY BITS!
LIBRARY
ULTRA-MEGA™
I love the library! I won't bok for you!
I HAVE WAYS OF MAKING YOU BOK!

Just then, Egg Drop jumped out. He tossed a Drumstick of Doom to Kung Pow Chicken.

The hero caught it in his beak and smashed the claw! He was free!

BOOM!!!!

Dr. Screech flung his arms and legs out wide. He opened his flight suit to escape. But Kung Pow Chicken was ready with his Beak-A-Rang. He plucked Dr. Screech right out of the sky!

BEAK-A-RANG!

The next morning, Mrs. Blue was on the phone with Uncle Quack. She squawked excitedly and then hung up.

cool horns

Cyndi Marko lives in Canada with her family.

When Cyndi was younger, she liked to sing loudly in the backseat of her mom's car. Her two older brothers would always plug their ears. In her yearbook, one classmate said that Cyndi's singing was her "pet peeve." But still . . . Cyndi kept singing. And singing. And singing. She didn't become a famous singer (at least, not yet!). She still loves to sing as loudly as she can though— especially while drawing super chickens.

Kung Pow Chicken is Cyndi's first children's book series.

Sketchbook of super chickens

singing machine

KUNG POW CHICKEN ★

Prove your superhero know-how!

What are some of Gordon's superpowers? Name three!

A compound word is made up of two words that come together to make one new word. Break these compound words into two words to figure out their meanings: *superpower*, *newspaper*, and *rooftops*.

Benny tells Gordon that, "a true hero helps out—no matter what other chickens say about him." Is this good advice? Why or why not?

What is Dr. Screech's evil plan?

Sam Snood does not believe Kung Pow Chicken is a hero. Pretend you are a reporter who believes he <u>is</u> a hero. Write an article about how he saved Honey Comb.